MY LITTLE PONY
PONY TALES

featuring RAINBOW DASH

STORY BY **Ryan K. Lindsay**

ART and COLORS BY **Tony Fleecs**

LETTERS BY **Neil Uyetake**

 Spotlight IDW

ABDOPUBLISHING.COM

Reinforced library bound edition published in 2015 by Spotlight,
a division of ABDO, PO Box 398166, Minneapolis, Minnesota 55439.
Spotlight produces high-quality reinforced library bound editions for
schools and libraries. Published by agreement with IDW.

Printed in the United States of America, North Mankato, Minnesota.
112014
012015

THIS BOOK CONTAINS
RECYCLED MATERIALS

LIBRARY OF CONGRESS CATALOGING-IN-PUBLICATION DATA

Lindsay, Ryan K.
  Rainbow Dash / writer, Ryan K. Lindsay ; artist, Tony Fleecs. -- Reinforced
library bound edition.
      pages cm. -- (My little pony. Pony tales)
  Summary: "Rainbow Dash battles a Cloud of Sadness"-- Provided by
publisher.
  ISBN 978-1-61479-334-2
1. Graphic novels. I. Fleecs, Tony, 1979- illustrator. II. Title.
  PZ7.7.L556Rai 2015
  741.5'973--dc23

                              2014036757

Spotlight

A Division of ABDO
abdopublishing.com

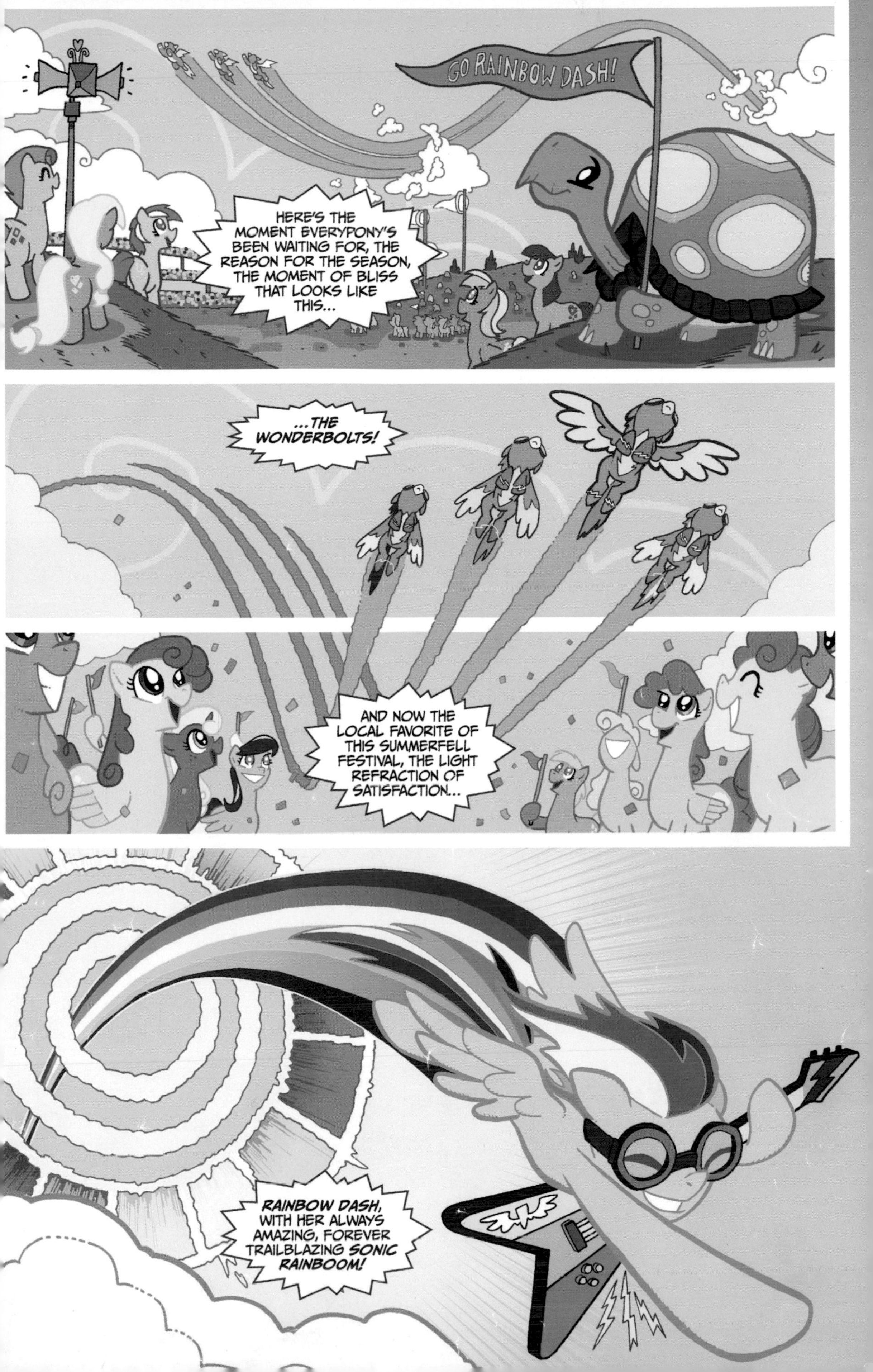
GO RAINBOW DASH!
HERE'S THE MOMENT EVERYPONY'S BEEN WAITING FOR, THE REASON FOR THE SEASON, THE MOMENT OF BLISS THAT LOOKS LIKE THIS...
...THE WONDERBOLTS!
AND NOW THE LOCAL FAVORITE OF THIS SUMMERFELL FESTIVAL, THE LIGHT REFRACTION OF SATISFACTION...
RAINBOW DASH, WITH HER ALWAYS AMAZING, FOREVER TRAILBLAZING SONIC RAINBOOM!

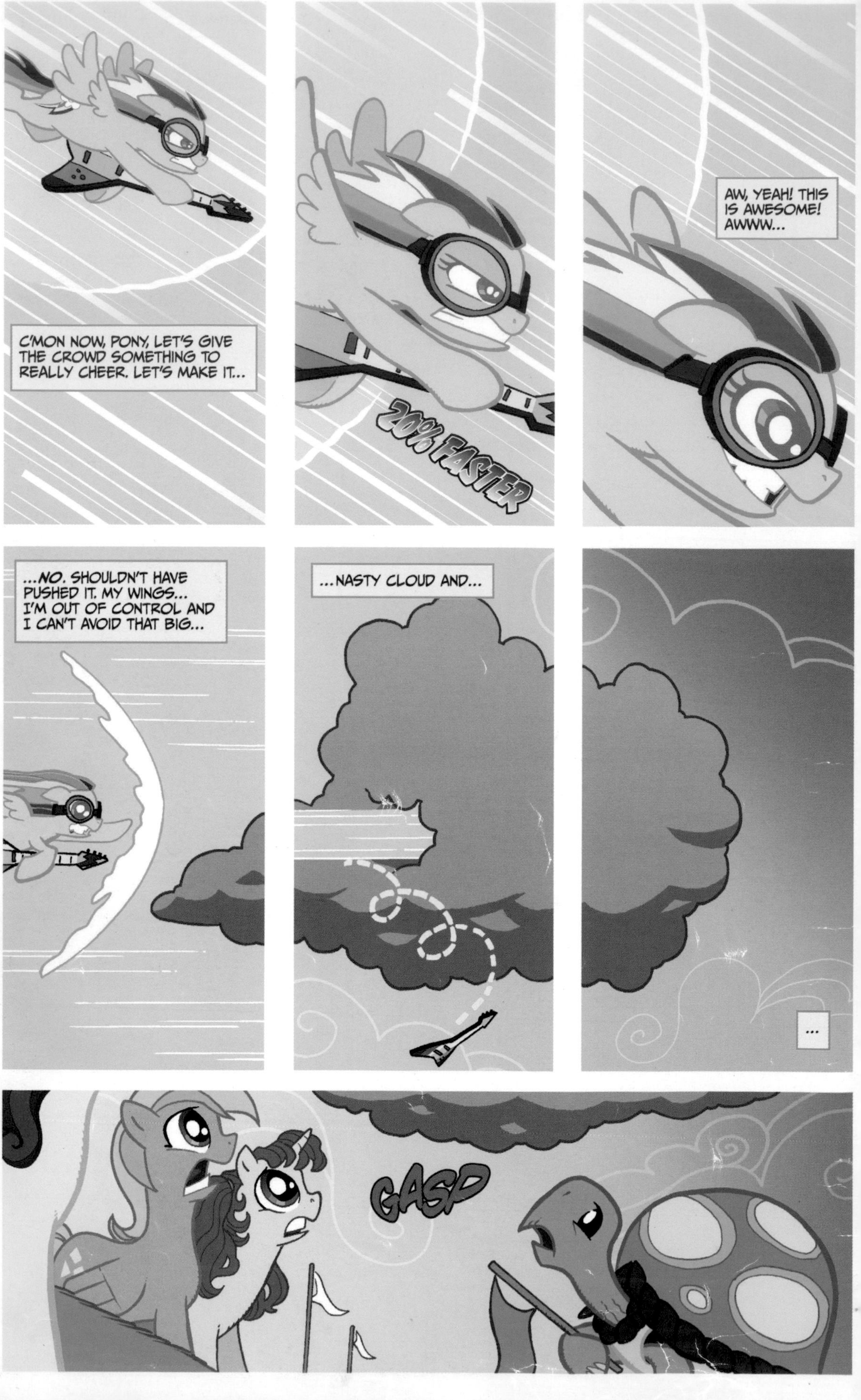
C'MON NOW, PONY, LET'S GIVE THE CROWD SOMETHING TO REALLY CHEER. LET'S MAKE IT...
20% FASTER
AW, YEAH! THIS IS AWESOME! AWWW...
...NO. SHOULDN'T HAVE PUSHED IT. MY WINGS... I'M OUT OF CONTROL AND I CAN'T AVOID THAT BIG...
...NASTY CLOUD AND...
...
GASP

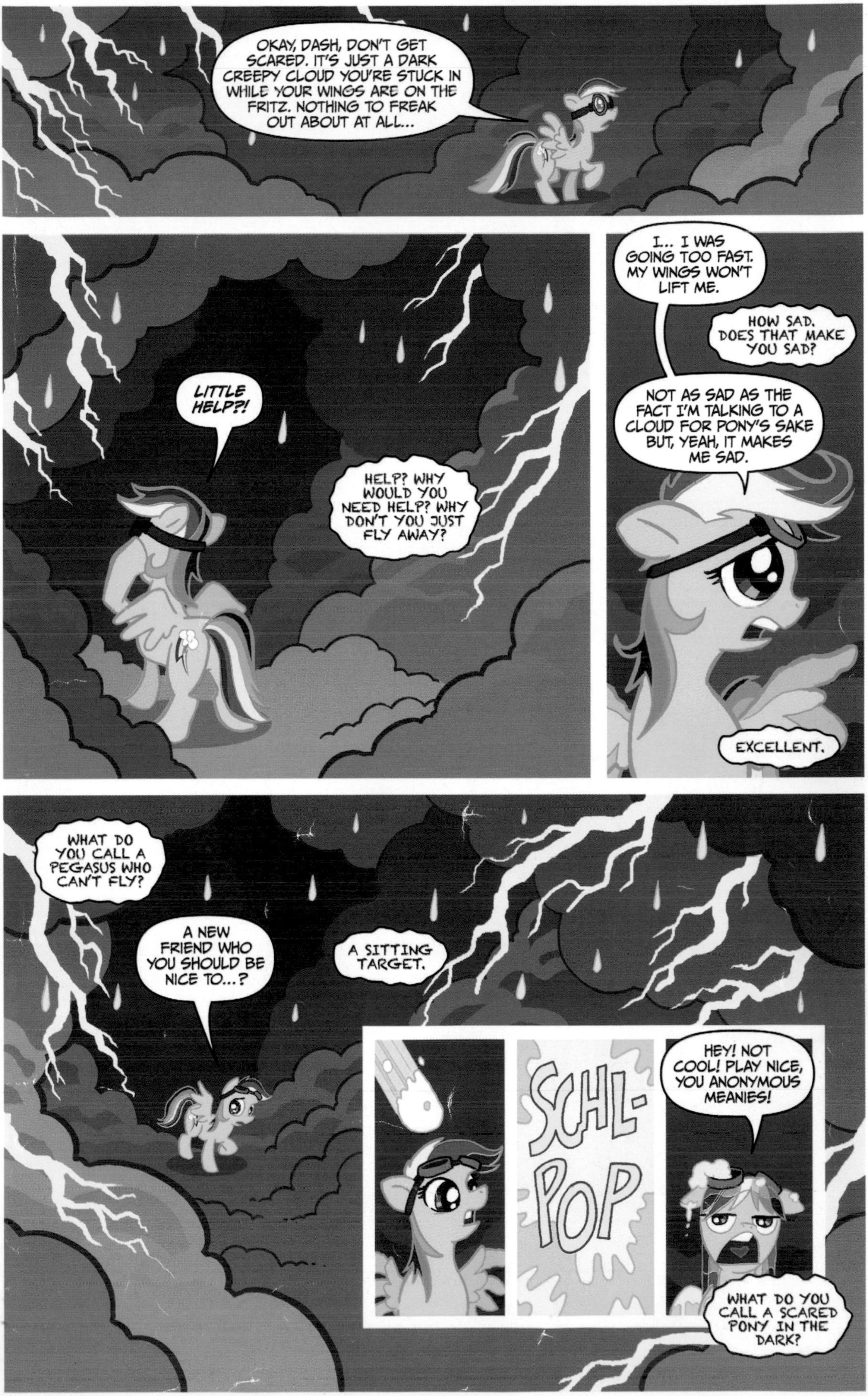
OKAY, DASH, DON'T GET SCARED. IT'S JUST A DARK CREEPY CLOUD YOU'RE STUCK IN WHILE YOUR WINGS ARE ON THE FRITZ. NOTHING TO FREAK OUT ABOUT AT ALL...
LITTLE HELP?!
HELP? WHY WOULD YOU NEED HELP? WHY DON'T YOU JUST FLY AWAY?
I... I WAS GOING TOO FAST. MY WINGS WON'T LIFT ME.
HOW SAD. DOES THAT MAKE YOU SAD?
NOT AS SAD AS THE FACT I'M TALKING TO A CLOUD FOR PONY'S SAKE BUT, YEAH, IT MAKES ME SAD.
EXCELLENT.
WHAT DO YOU CALL A PEGASUS WHO CAN'T FLY?
A NEW FRIEND WHO YOU SHOULD BE NICE TO...?
A SITTING TARGET.
SCHL-POP
HEY! NOT COOL! PLAY NICE, YOU ANONYMOUS MEANIES!
WHAT DO YOU CALL A SCARED PONY IN THE DARK?

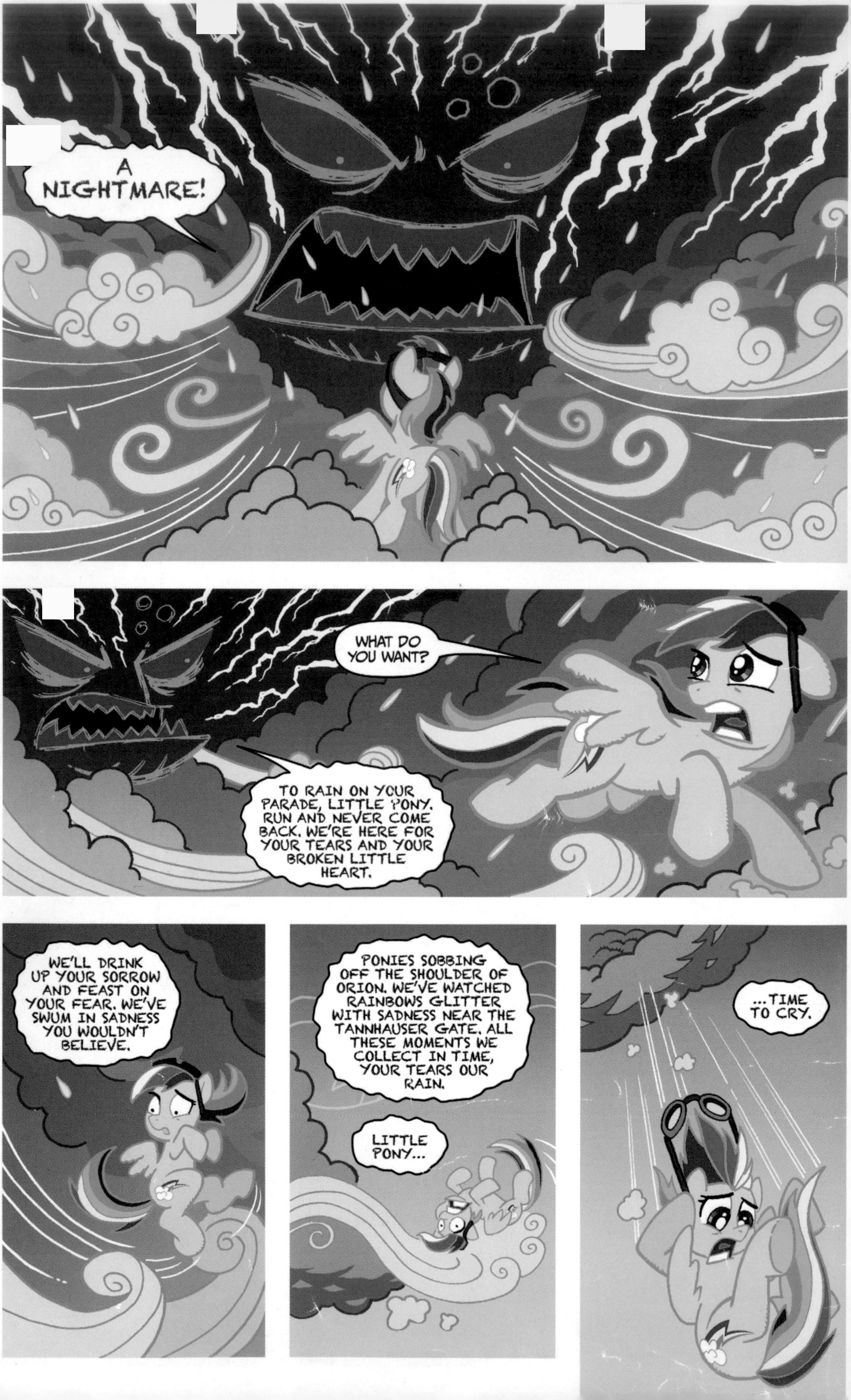
A NIGHTMARE!
WHAT DO YOU WANT?
TO RAIN ON YOUR PARADE, LITTLE PONY. RUN AND NEVER COME BACK. WE'RE HERE FOR YOUR TEARS AND YOUR BROKEN LITTLE HEART.
WE'LL DRINK UP YOUR SORROW AND FEAST ON YOUR FEAR. WE'VE SWUM IN SADNESS YOU WOULDN'T BELIEVE.
PONIES SOBBING OFF THE SHOULDER OF ORION. WE'VE WATCHED RAINBOWS GLITTER WITH SADNESS NEAR THE TANNHAUSER GATE. ALL THESE MOMENTS WE COLLECT IN TIME, YOUR TEARS OUR RAIN.
LITTLE PONY...
...TIME TO CRY.

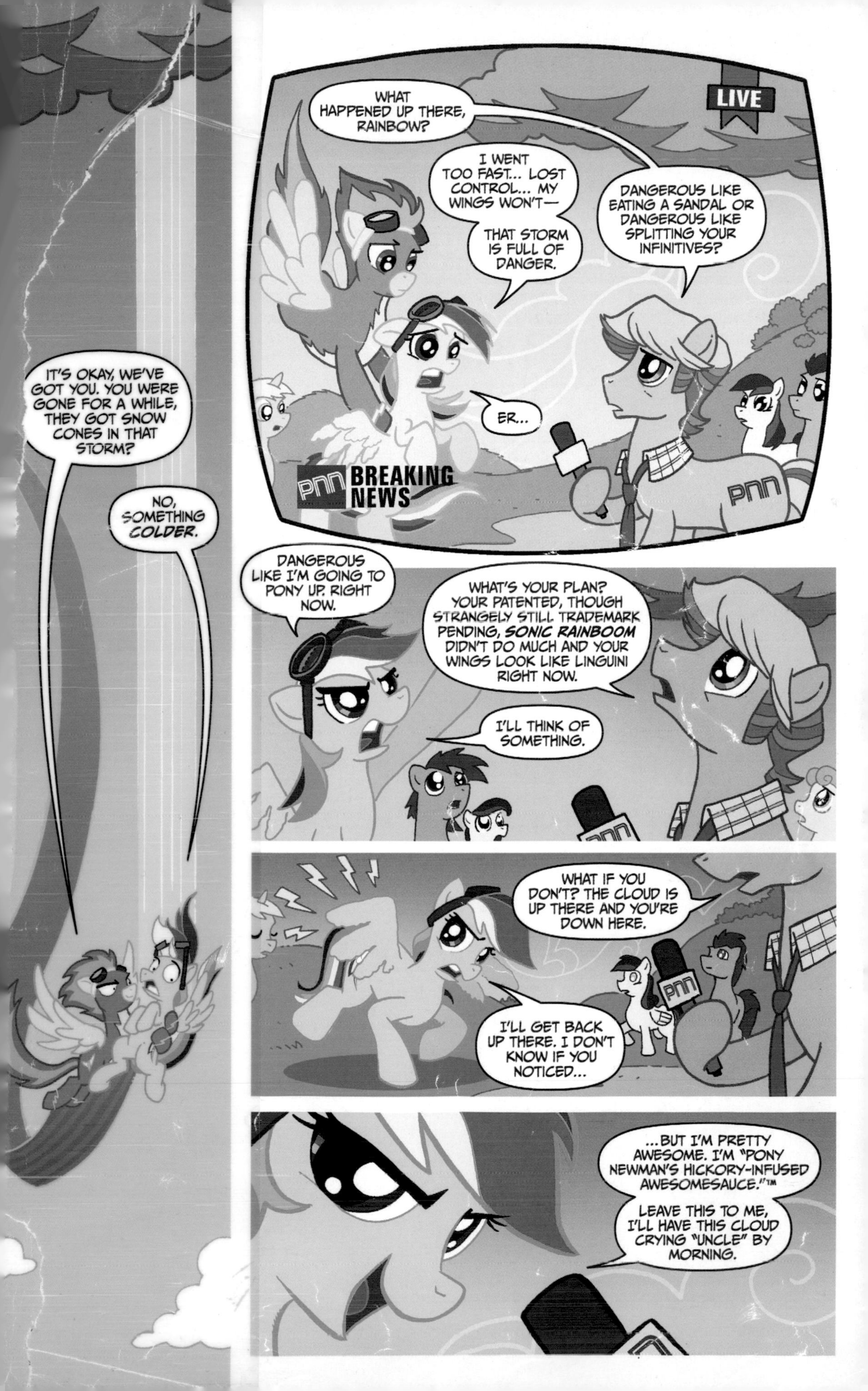
IT'S OKAY, WE'VE GOT YOU. YOU WERE GONE FOR A WHILE, THEY GOT SNOW CONES IN THAT STORM?
NO, SOMETHING *COLDER*.
LIVE
WHAT HAPPENED UP THERE, RAINBOW?
I WENT TOO FAST... LOST CONTROL... MY WINGS WON'T—
THAT STORM IS FULL OF DANGER.
DANGEROUS LIKE EATING A SANDAL OR DANGEROUS LIKE SPLITTING YOUR INFINITIVES?
ER...
PNN BREAKING NEWS
PNN
DANGEROUS LIKE I'M GOING TO PONY UP. RIGHT NOW.
WHAT'S YOUR PLAN? YOUR PATENTED, THOUGH STRANGELY STILL TRADEMARK PENDING, *SONIC RAINBOOM* DIDN'T DO MUCH AND YOUR WINGS LOOK LIKE LINGUINI RIGHT NOW.
I'LL THINK OF SOMETHING.
WHAT IF YOU DON'T? THE CLOUD IS UP THERE AND YOU'RE DOWN HERE.
I'LL GET BACK UP THERE. I DON'T KNOW IF YOU NOTICED...
...BUT I'M PRETTY AWESOME. I'M "PONY NEWMAN'S HICKORY-INFUSED AWESOMESAUCE."™
LEAVE THIS TO ME, I'LL HAVE THIS CLOUD CRYING "UNCLE" BY MORNING.

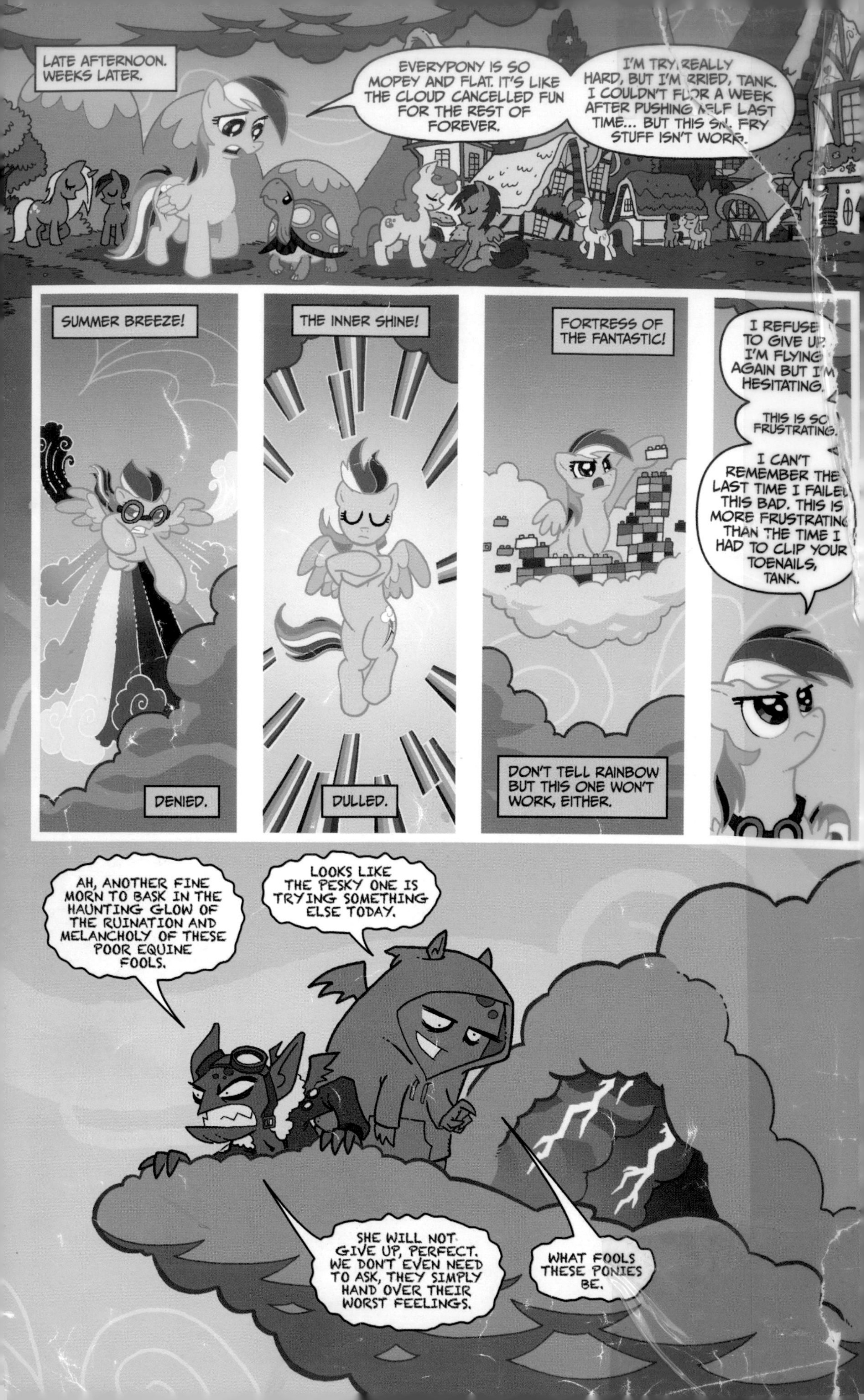

LATE AFTERNOON. WEEKS LATER.
EVERYPONY IS SO MOPEY AND FLAT. IT'S LIKE THE CLOUD CANCELLED FUN FOR THE REST OF FOREVER.
I'M TRY REALLY HARD, BUT I'M RRIED, TANK. I COULDN'T FL OR A WEEK AFTER PUSHING ELF LAST TIME... BUT THIS S. FRY STUFF ISN'T WOR
SUMMER BREEZE!
DENIED.
THE INNER SHINE!
DULLED.
FORTRESS OF THE FANTASTIC!
DON'T TELL RAINBOW BUT THIS ONE WON'T WORK, EITHER.
I REFUSE TO GIVE UP. I'M FLYING AGAIN BUT I'M HESITATING.
THIS IS SO FRUSTRATING.
I CAN'T REMEMBER THE LAST TIME I FAILED THIS BAD. THIS IS MORE FRUSTRATING THAN THE TIME I HAD TO CLIP YOUR TOENAILS, TANK.
AH, ANOTHER FINE MORN TO BASK IN THE HAUNTING GLOW OF THE RUINATION AND MELANCHOLY OF THESE POOR EQUINE FOOLS.
LOOKS LIKE THE PESKY ONE IS TRYING SOMETHING ELSE TODAY.
SHE WILL NOT GIVE UP, PERFECT. WE DON'T EVEN NEED TO ASK, THEY SIMPLY HAND OVER THEIR WORST FEELINGS.
WHAT FOOLS THESE PONIES BE.

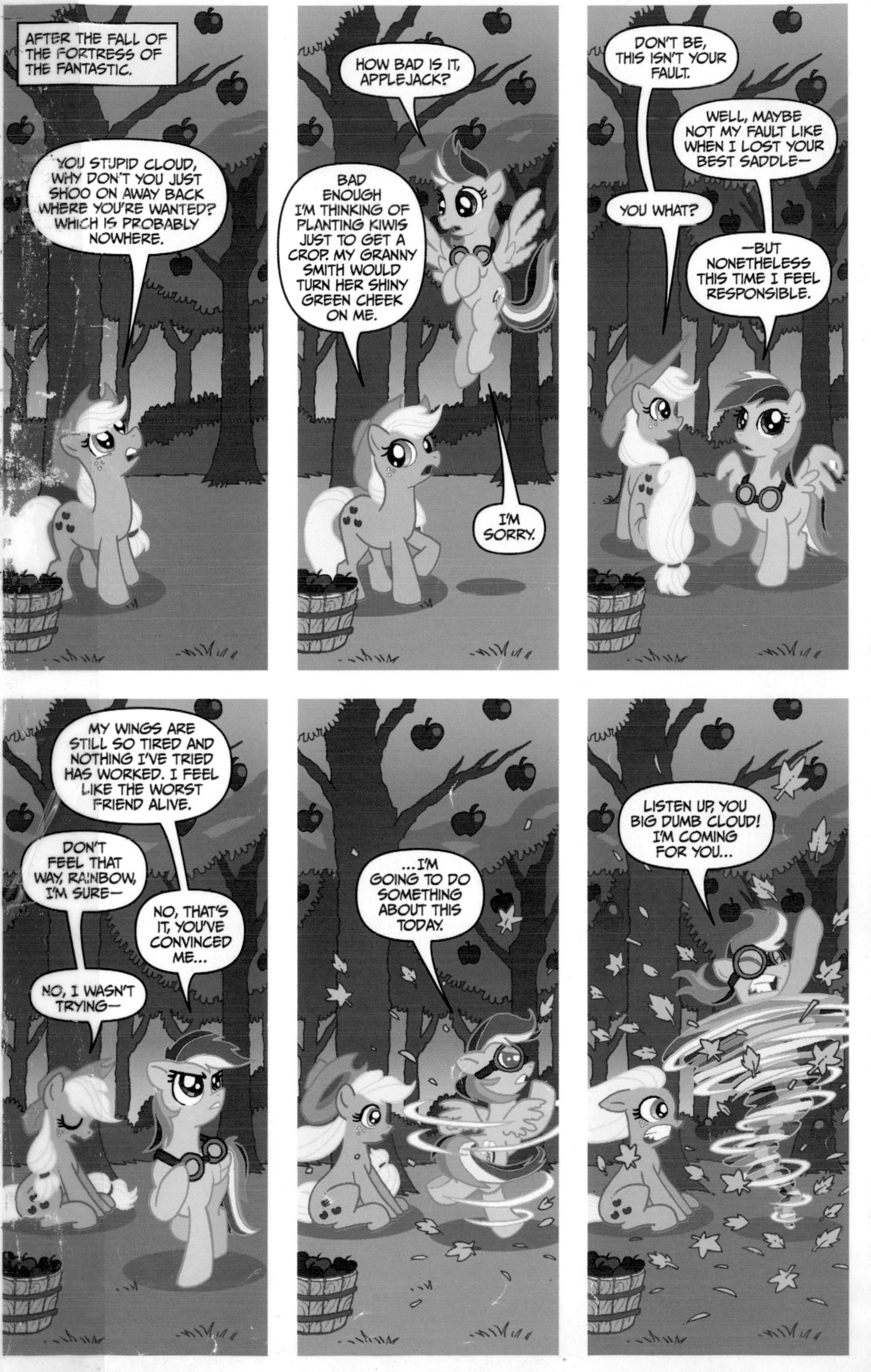
AFTER THE FALL OF THE FORTRESS OF THE FANTASTIC.
YOU STUPID CLOUD, WHY DON'T YOU JUST SHOO ON AWAY BACK WHERE YOU'RE WANTED? WHICH IS PROBABLY NOWHERE.
HOW BAD IS IT, APPLEJACK?
BAD ENOUGH I'M THINKING OF PLANTING KIWIS JUST TO GET A CROP. MY GRANNY SMITH WOULD TURN HER SHINY GREEN CHEEK ON ME.
I'M SORRY.
DON'T BE, THIS ISN'T YOUR FAULT.
WELL, MAYBE NOT MY FAULT LIKE WHEN I LOST YOUR BEST SADDLE—
YOU WHAT?
—BUT NONETHELESS THIS TIME I FEEL RESPONSIBLE.
MY WINGS ARE STILL SO TIRED AND NOTHING I'VE TRIED HAS WORKED. I FEEL LIKE THE WORST FRIEND ALIVE.
DON'T FEEL THAT WAY, RAINBOW, I'M SURE—
NO, THAT'S IT, YOU'VE CONVINCED ME...
NO, I WASN'T TRYING—
...I'M GOING TO DO SOMETHING ABOUT THIS TODAY.
LISTEN UP, YOU BIG DUMB CLOUD! I'M COMING FOR YOU...

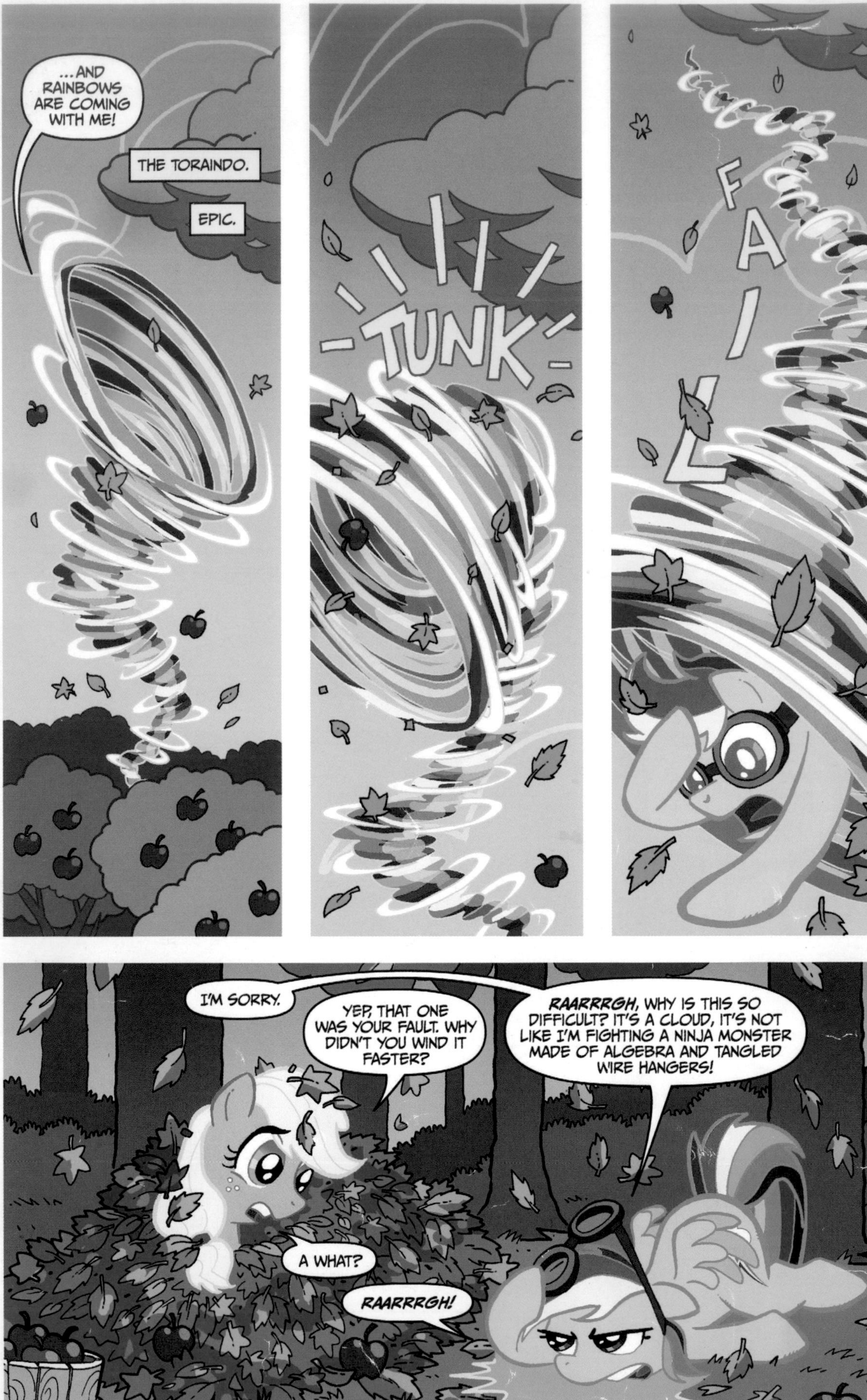
...AND RAINBOWS ARE COMING WITH ME!
THE TORAINDO.
EPIC.
TUNK
FAIL
I'M SORRY.
YEP, THAT ONE WAS YOUR FAULT. WHY DIDN'T YOU WIND IT FASTER?
RAARRRGH, WHY IS THIS SO DIFFICULT? IT'S A CLOUD, IT'S NOT LIKE I'M FIGHTING A NINJA MONSTER MADE OF ALGEBRA AND TANGLED WIRE HANGERS!
A WHAT?
RAARRRGH!

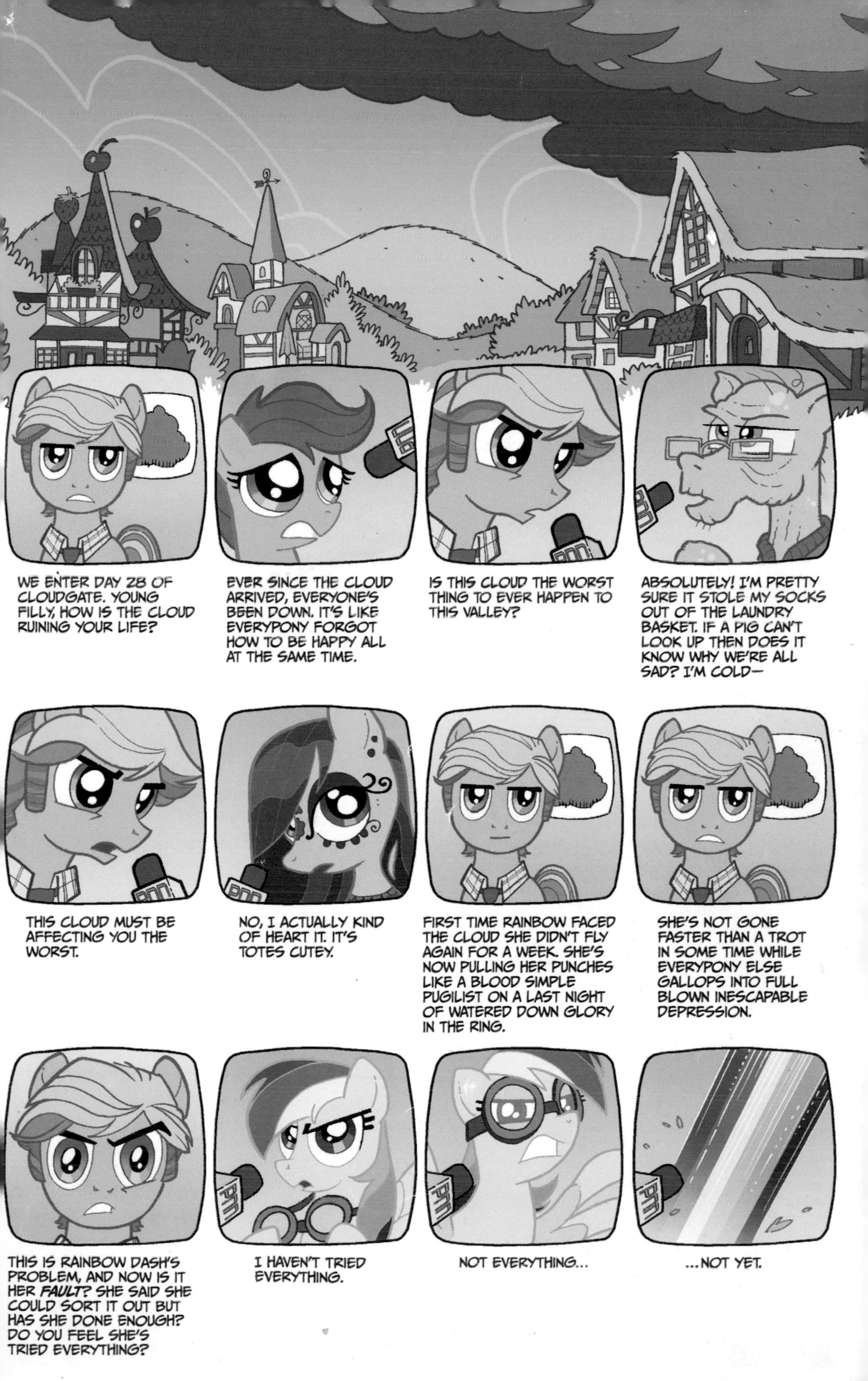

WE ENTER DAY 28 OF CLOUDGATE. YOUNG FILLY, HOW IS THE CLOUD RUINING YOUR LIFE?
EVER SINCE THE CLOUD ARRIVED, EVERYONE'S BEEN DOWN. IT'S LIKE EVERYPONY FORGOT HOW TO BE HAPPY ALL AT THE SAME TIME.
IS THIS CLOUD THE WORST THING TO EVER HAPPEN TO THIS VALLEY?
ABSOLUTELY! I'M PRETTY SURE IT STOLE MY SOCKS OUT OF THE LAUNDRY BASKET. IF A PIG CAN'T LOOK UP THEN DOES IT KNOW WHY WE'RE ALL SAD? I'M COLD—
THIS CLOUD MUST BE AFFECTING YOU THE WORST.
NO, I ACTUALLY KIND OF HEART IT. IT'S TOTES CUTEY.
FIRST TIME RAINBOW FACED THE CLOUD SHE DIDN'T FLY AGAIN FOR A WEEK. SHE'S NOW PULLING HER PUNCHES LIKE A BLOOD SIMPLE PUGILIST ON A LAST NIGHT OF WATERED DOWN GLORY IN THE RING.
SHE'S NOT GONE FASTER THAN A TROT IN SOME TIME WHILE EVERYPONY ELSE GALLOPS INTO FULL BLOWN INESCAPABLE DEPRESSION.
THIS IS RAINBOW DASH'S PROBLEM, AND NOW IS IT HER *FAULT*? SHE SAID SHE COULD SORT IT OUT BUT HAS SHE DONE ENOUGH? DO YOU FEEL SHE'S TRIED EVERYTHING?
I HAVEN'T TRIED EVERYTHING.
NOT EVERYTHING...
...NOT YET.

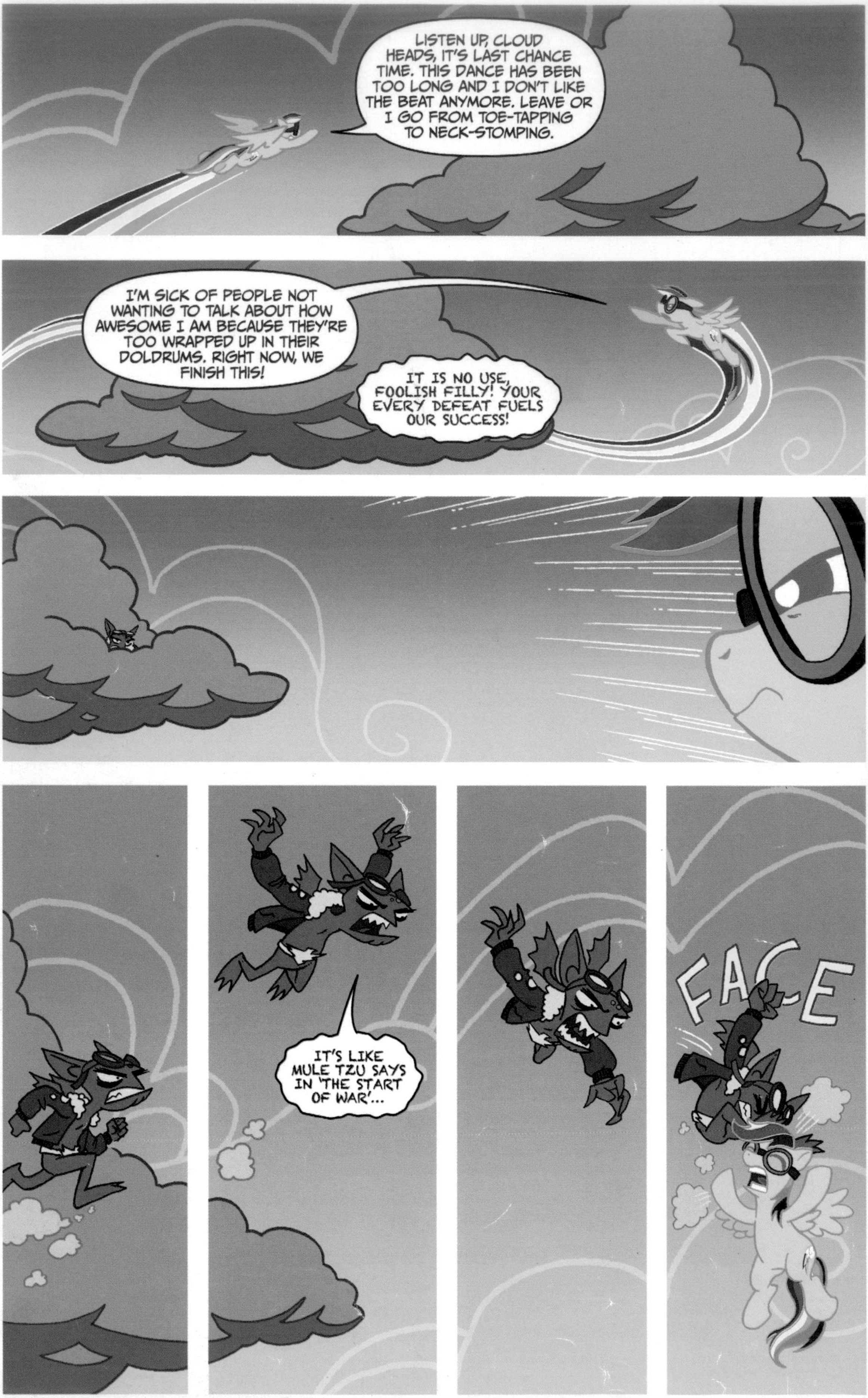
LISTEN UP, CLOUD HEADS, IT'S LAST CHANCE TIME. THIS DANCE HAS BEEN TOO LONG AND I DON'T LIKE THE BEAT ANYMORE. LEAVE OR I GO FROM TOE-TAPPING TO NECK-STOMPING.
I'M SICK OF PEOPLE NOT WANTING TO TALK ABOUT HOW AWESOME I AM BECAUSE THEY'RE TOO WRAPPED UP IN THEIR DOLDRUMS. RIGHT NOW, WE FINISH THIS!
IT IS NO USE, FOOLISH FILLY! YOUR EVERY DEFEAT FUELS OUR SUCCESS!
IT'S LIKE MULE TZU SAYS IN 'THE START OF WAR'...
FACE

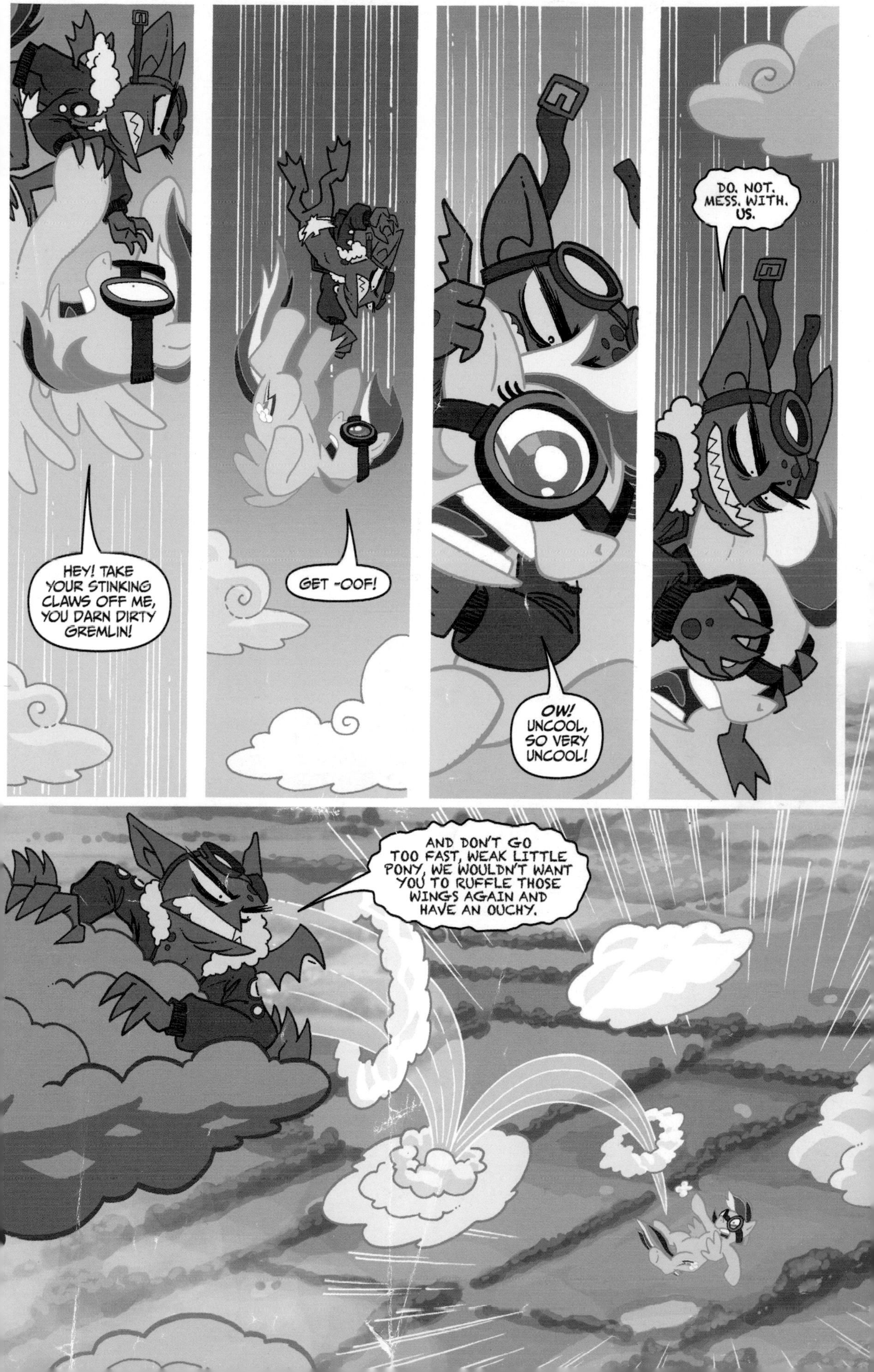

HEY! TAKE YOUR STINKING CLAWS OFF ME, YOU DARN DIRTY GREMLIN!
GET -OOF!
OW! UNCOOL, SO VERY UNCOOL!
DO. NOT. MESS. WITH. US.
AND DON'T GO TOO FAST, WEAK LITTLE PONY, WE WOULDN'T WANT YOU TO RUFFLE THOSE WINGS AGAIN AND HAVE AN OUCHY.

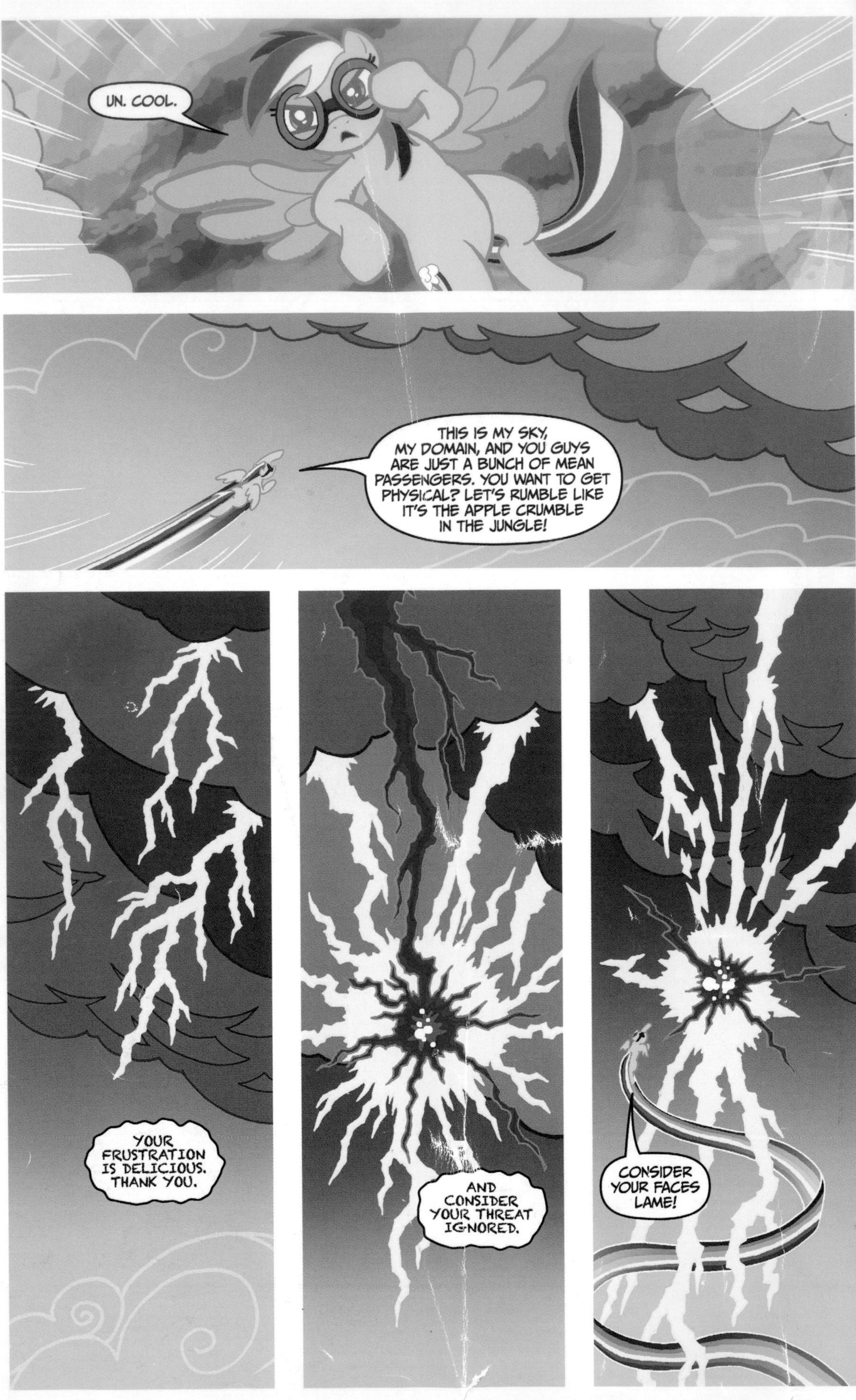
UN. COOL.
THIS IS MY SKY, MY DOMAIN, AND YOU GUYS ARE JUST A BUNCH OF MEAN PASSENGERS. YOU WANT TO GET PHYSICAL? LET'S RUMBLE LIKE IT'S THE APPLE CRUMBLE IN THE JUNGLE!
YOUR FRUSTRATION IS DELICIOUS. THANK YOU.
AND CONSIDER YOUR THREAT IGNORED.
CONSIDER YOUR FACES LAME!

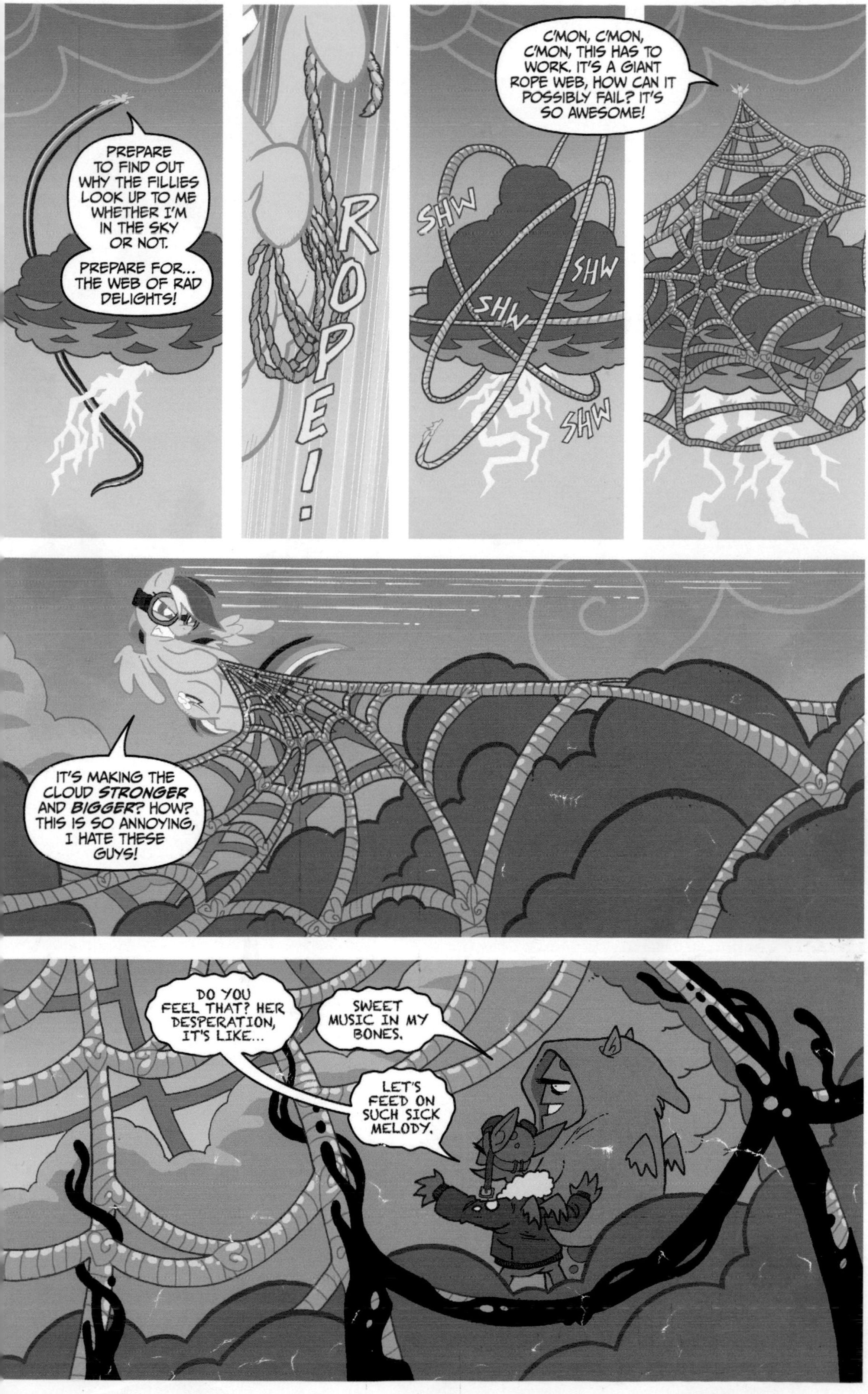
PREPARE TO FIND OUT WHY THE FILLIES LOOK UP TO ME WHETHER I'M IN THE SKY OR NOT.
PREPARE FOR... THE WEB OF RAD DELIGHTS!
ROPE!
C'MON, C'MON, C'MON, THIS HAS TO WORK. IT'S A GIANT ROPE WEB, HOW CAN IT POSSIBLY FAIL? IT'S SO AWESOME!
SHW
SHW
SHW
SHW
IT'S MAKING THE CLOUD STRONGER AND BIGGER? HOW? THIS IS SO ANNOYING, I HATE THESE GUYS!
DO YOU FEEL THAT? HER DESPERATION, IT'S LIKE...
SWEET MUSIC IN MY BONES.
LET'S FEED ON SUCH SICK MELODY.

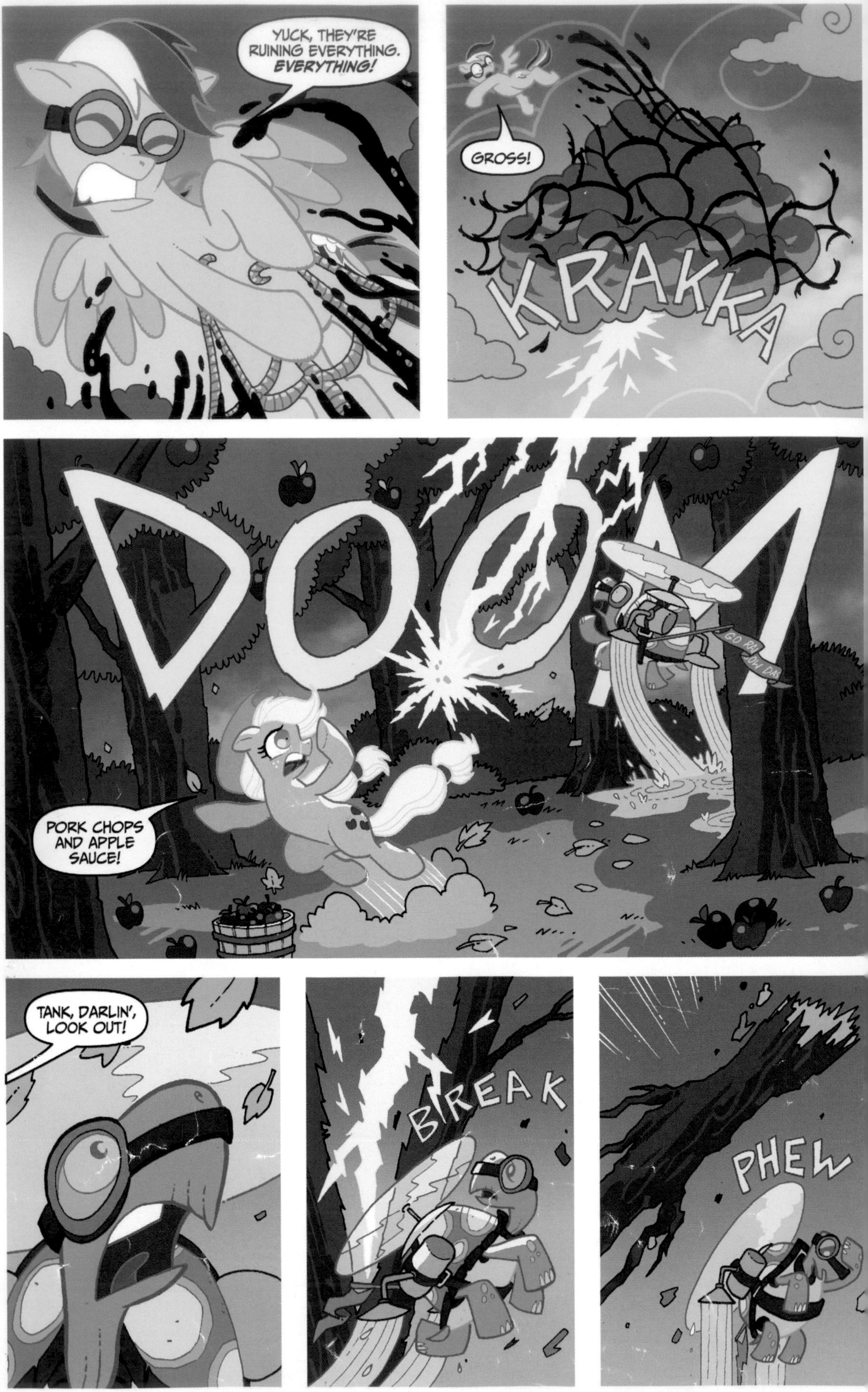
YUCK, THEY'RE RUINING EVERYTHING. *EVERYTHING!*
GROSS!
KRAKKA
DOOM
PORK CHOPS AND APPLE SAUCE!
TANK, DARLIN', LOOK OUT!
BREAK
PHEW

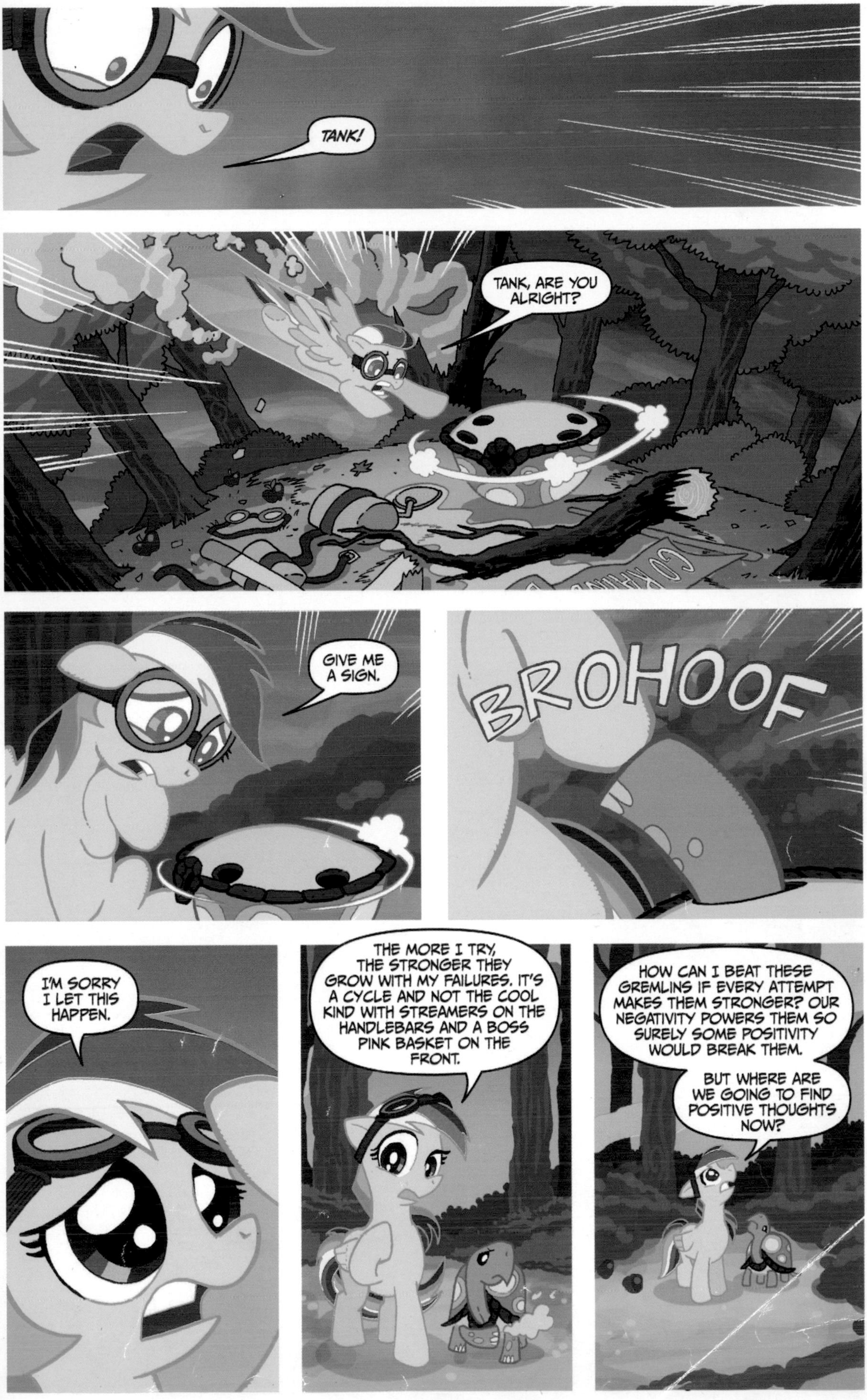
TANK!
TANK, ARE YOU ALRIGHT?
GIVE ME A SIGN.
BROHOOF
I'M SORRY I LET THIS HAPPEN.
THE MORE I TRY, THE STRONGER THEY GROW WITH MY FAILURES. IT'S A CYCLE AND NOT THE COOL KIND WITH STREAMERS ON THE HANDLEBARS AND A BOSS PINK BASKET ON THE FRONT.
HOW CAN I BEAT THESE GREMLINS IF EVERY ATTEMPT MAKES THEM STRONGER? OUR NEGATIVITY POWERS THEM SO SURELY SOME POSITIVITY WOULD BREAK THEM.
BUT WHERE ARE WE GOING TO FIND POSITIVE THOUGHTS NOW?

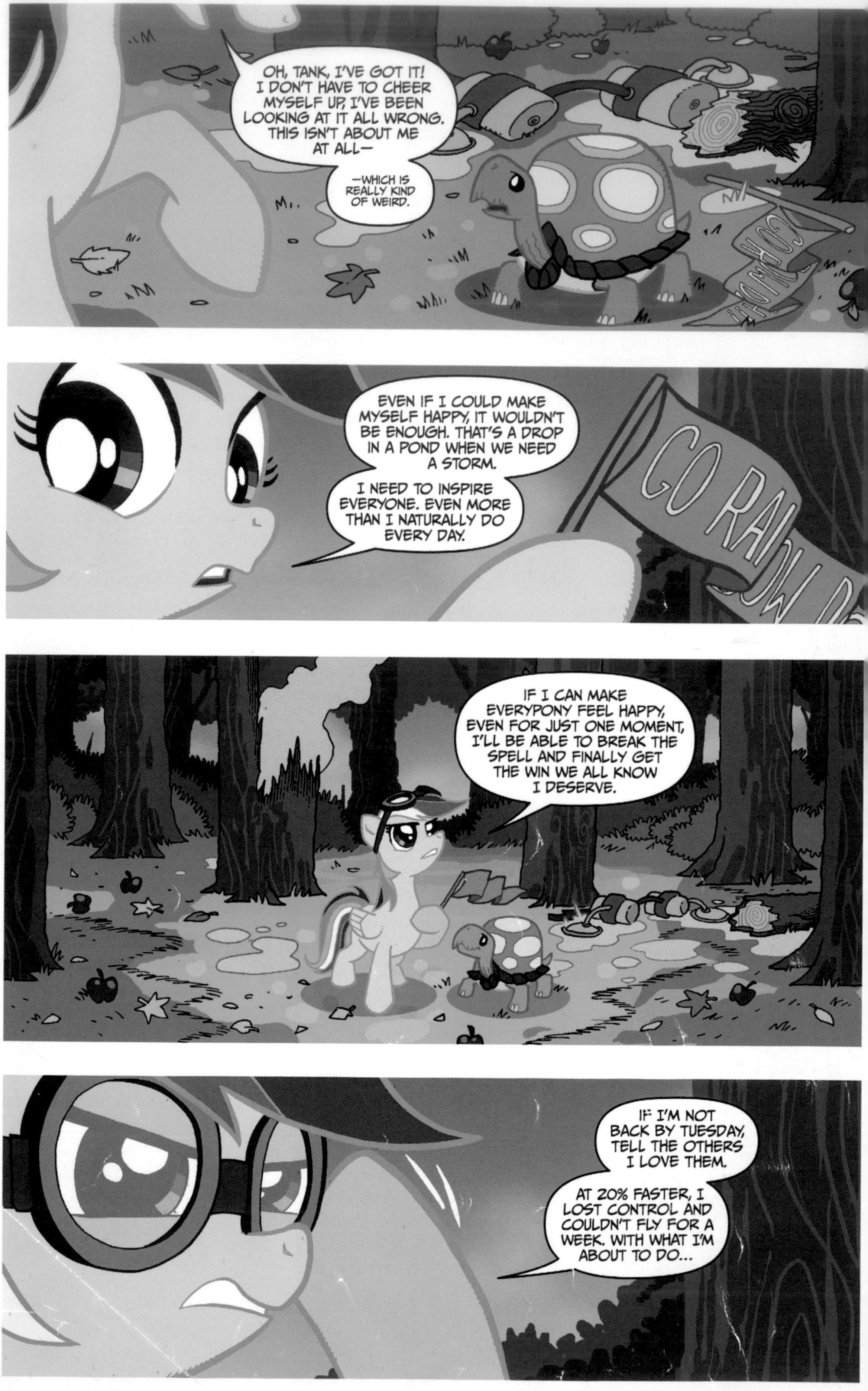
OH, TANK, I'VE GOT IT! I DON'T HAVE TO CHEER MYSELF UP, I'VE BEEN LOOKING AT IT ALL WRONG. THIS ISN'T ABOUT ME AT ALL—
—WHICH IS REALLY KIND OF WEIRD.
EVEN IF I COULD MAKE MYSELF HAPPY, IT WOULDN'T BE ENOUGH. THAT'S A DROP IN A POND WHEN WE NEED A STORM.
I NEED TO INSPIRE EVERYONE. EVEN MORE THAN I NATURALLY DO EVERY DAY.
IF I CAN MAKE EVERYPONY FEEL HAPPY, EVEN FOR JUST ONE MOMENT, I'LL BE ABLE TO BREAK THE SPELL AND FINALLY GET THE WIN WE ALL KNOW I DESERVE.
IF I'M NOT BACK BY TUESDAY, TELL THE OTHERS I LOVE THEM.
AT 20% FASTER, I LOST CONTROL AND COULDN'T FLY FOR A WEEK. WITH WHAT I'M ABOUT TO DO...

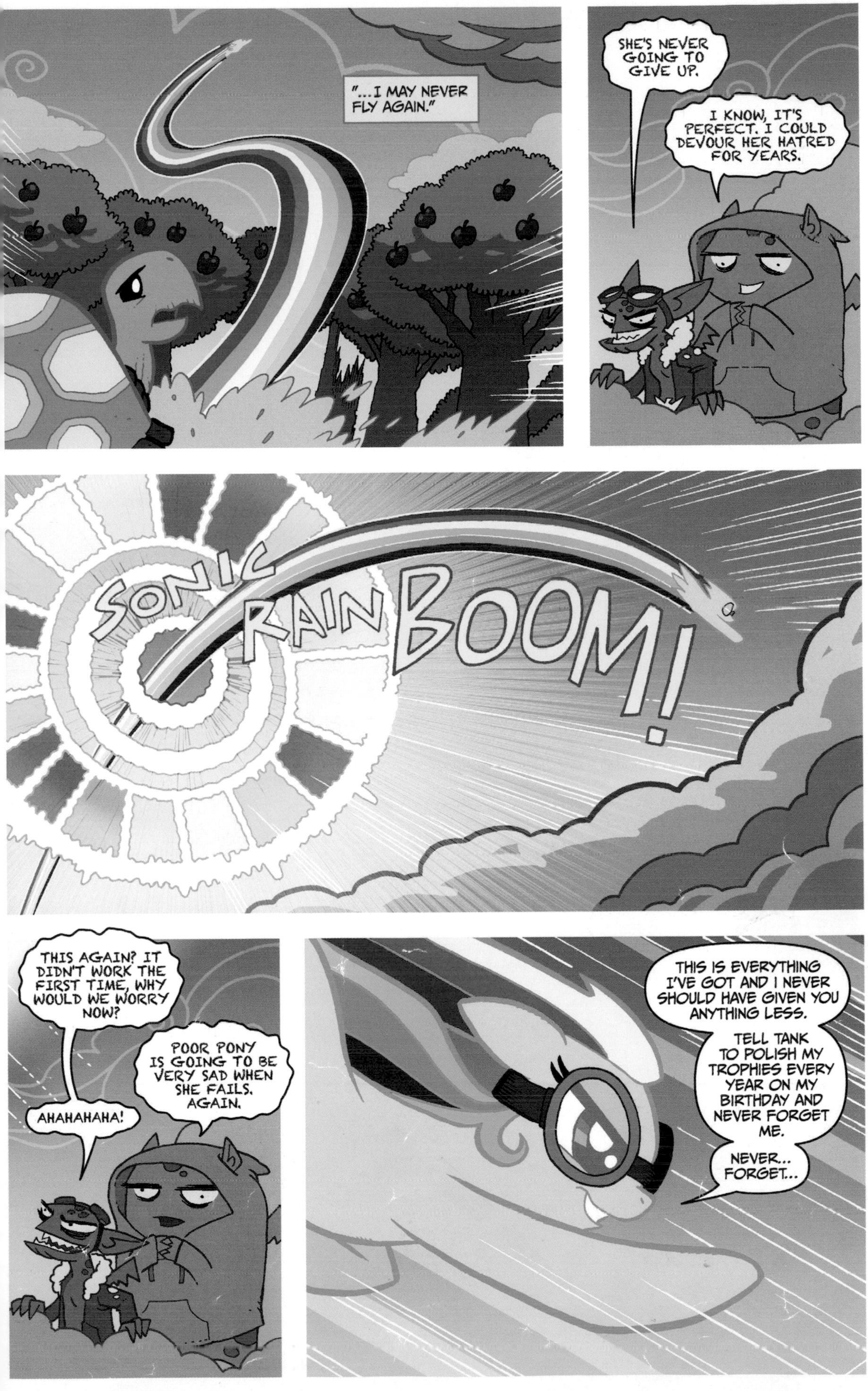
"...I MAY NEVER FLY AGAIN."
SHE'S NEVER GOING TO GIVE UP.
I KNOW, IT'S PERFECT. I COULD DEVOUR HER HATRED FOR YEARS.
SONIC RAINBOOM!
THIS AGAIN? IT DIDN'T WORK THE FIRST TIME, WHY WOULD WE WORRY NOW?
AHAHAHAHA!
POOR PONY IS GOING TO BE VERY SAD WHEN SHE FAILS. AGAIN.
THIS IS EVERYTHING I'VE GOT AND I NEVER SHOULD HAVE GIVEN YOU ANYTHING LESS.
TELL TANK TO POLISH MY TROPHIES EVERY YEAR ON MY BIRTHDAY AND NEVER FORGET ME.
NEVER... FORGET...

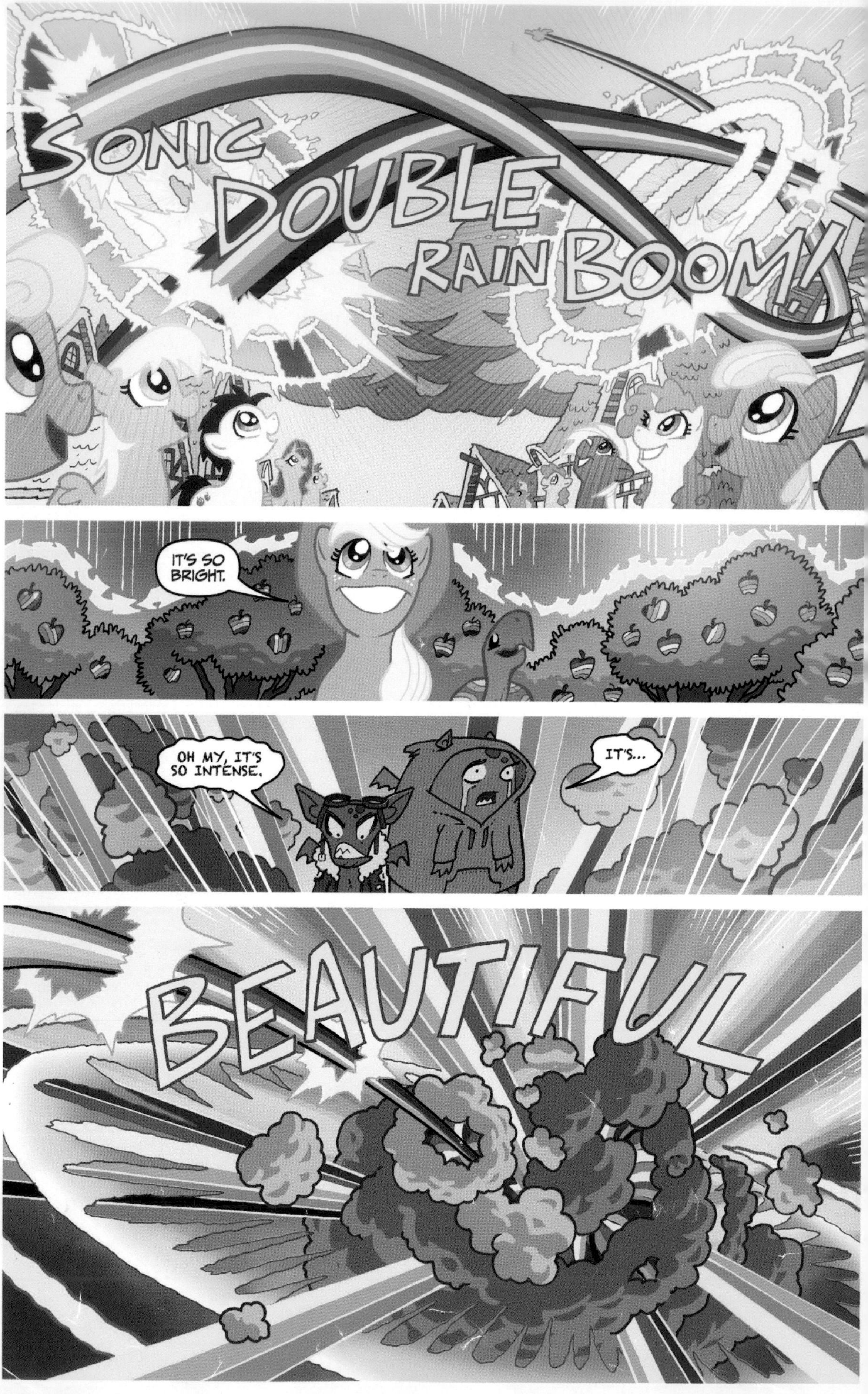
SONIC DOUBLE RAINBOOM!
IT'S SO BRIGHT.
OH MY, IT'S SO INTENSE.
IT'S...
BEAUTIFUL

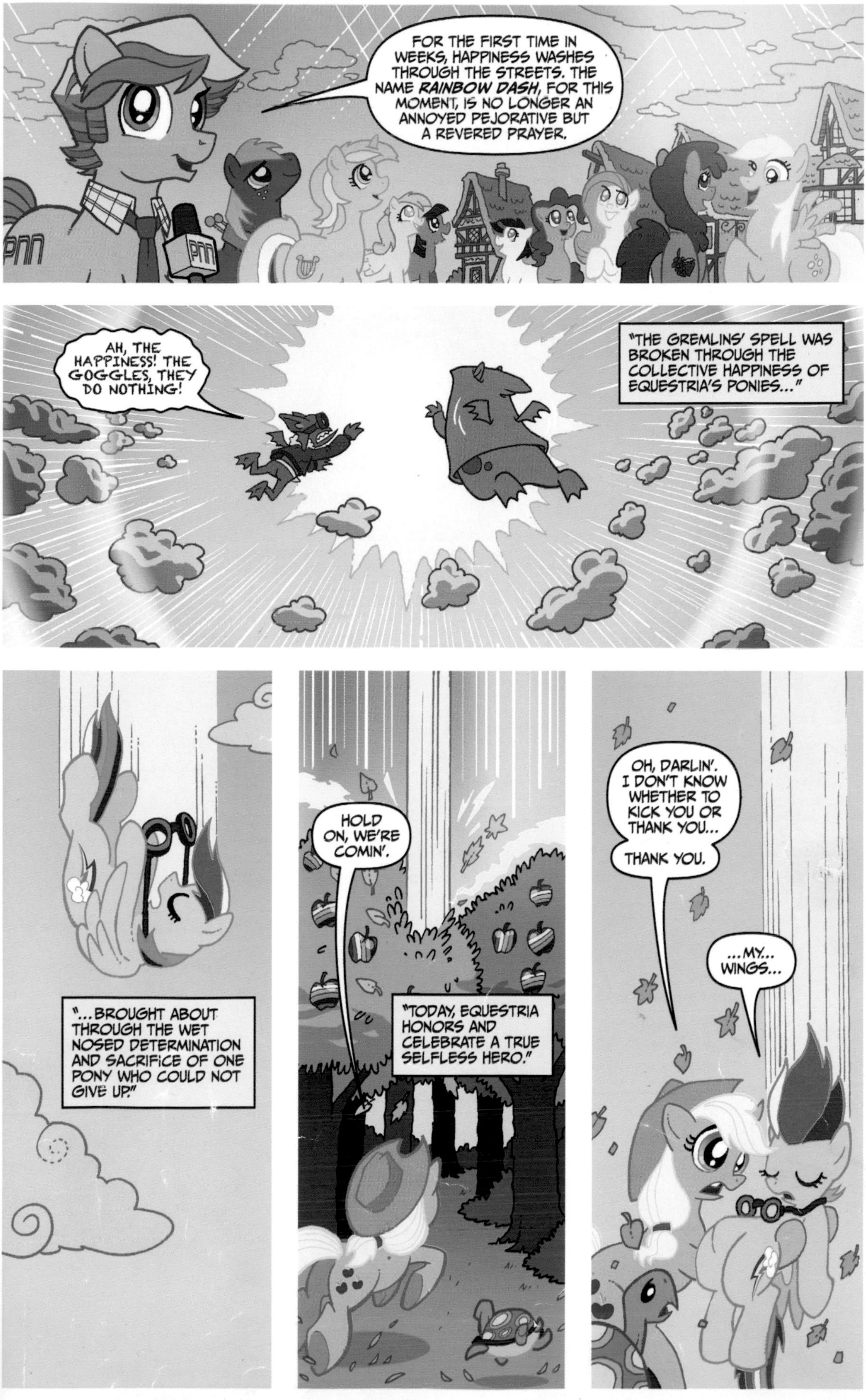

FOR THE FIRST TIME IN WEEKS, HAPPINESS WASHES THROUGH THE STREETS. THE NAME *RAINBOW DASH*, FOR THIS MOMENT, IS NO LONGER AN ANNOYED PEJORATIVE BUT A REVERED PRAYER.
PNN
PNN
AH, THE HAPPINESS! THE GOGGLES, THEY DO NOTHING!
"THE GREMLINS' SPELL WAS BROKEN THROUGH THE COLLECTIVE HAPPINESS OF EQUESTRIA'S PONIES..."
"...BROUGHT ABOUT THROUGH THE WET NOSED DETERMINATION AND SACRIFICE OF ONE PONY WHO COULD NOT GIVE UP."
HOLD ON, WE'RE COMIN'.
"TODAY, EQUESTRIA HONORS AND CELEBRATE A TRUE SELFLESS HERO."
OH, DARLIN'. I DON'T KNOW WHETHER TO KICK YOU OR THANK YOU...
THANK YOU.
...MY... WINGS...

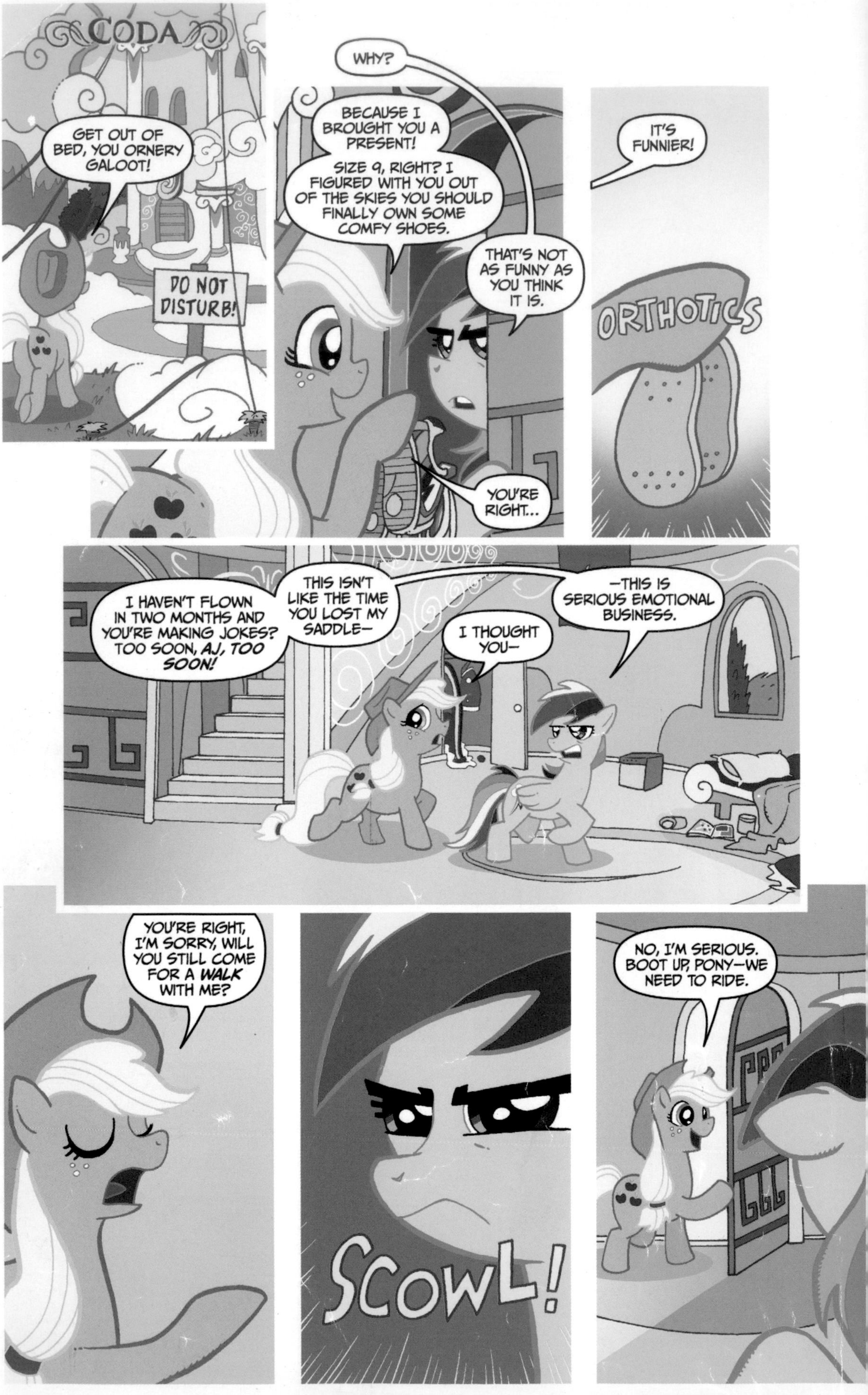
CODA
GET OUT OF BED, YOU ORNERY GALOOT!
DO NOT DISTURB!
WHY?
BECAUSE I BROUGHT YOU A PRESENT!
SIZE 9, RIGHT? I FIGURED WITH YOU OUT OF THE SKIES YOU SHOULD FINALLY OWN SOME COMFY SHOES.
THAT'S NOT AS FUNNY AS YOU THINK IT IS.
YOU'RE RIGHT...
IT'S FUNNIER!
ORTHOTICS
I HAVEN'T FLOWN IN TWO MONTHS AND YOU'RE MAKING JOKES? TOO SOON, AJ, TOO SOON!
THIS ISN'T LIKE THE TIME YOU LOST MY SADDLE—
I THOUGHT YOU—
—THIS IS SERIOUS EMOTIONAL BUSINESS.
YOU'RE RIGHT, I'M SORRY, WILL YOU STILL COME FOR A WALK WITH ME?
SCOWL!
NO, I'M SERIOUS. BOOT UP, PONY—WE NEED TO RIDE.

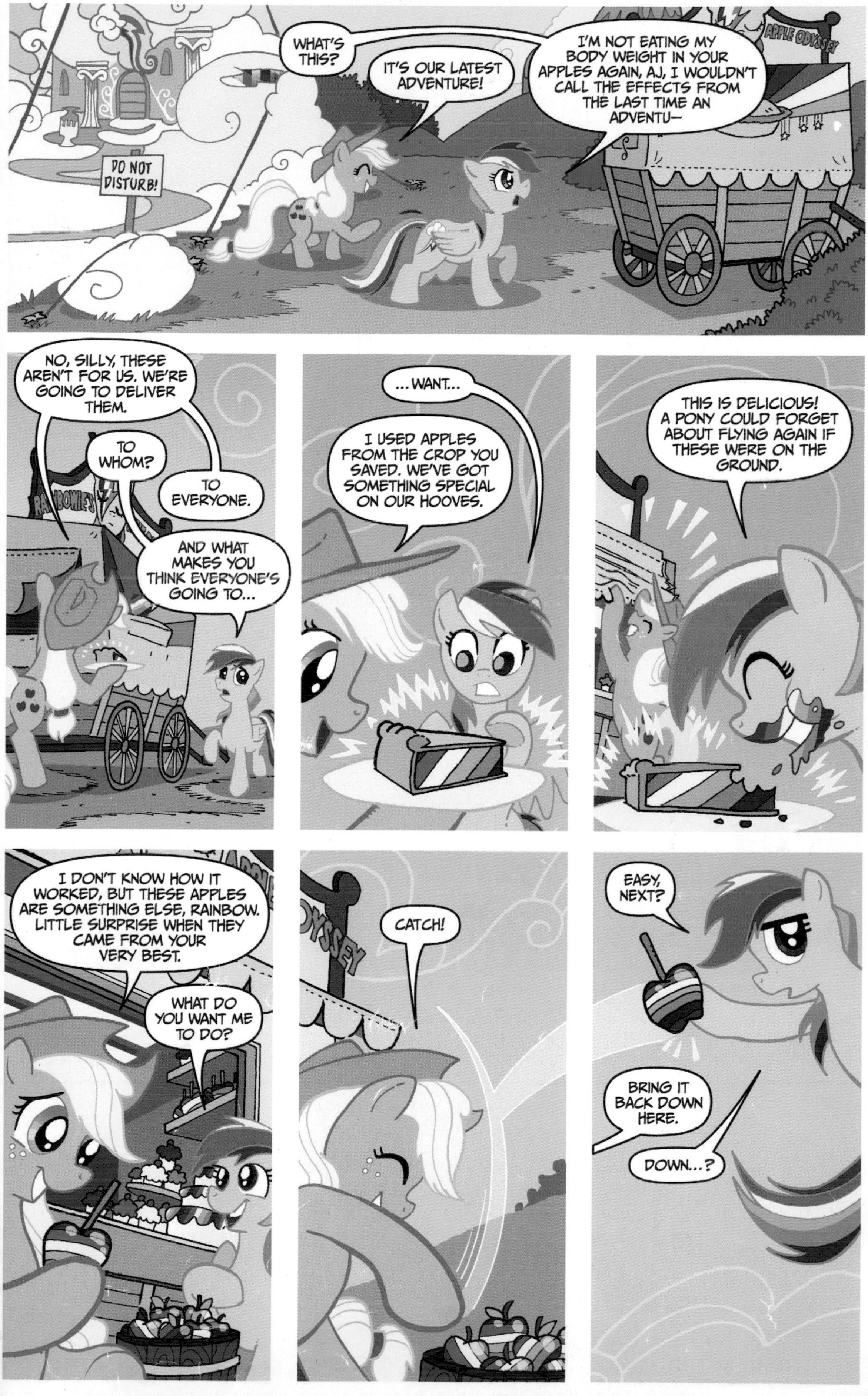
WHAT'S THIS?
IT'S OUR LATEST ADVENTURE!
I'M NOT EATING MY BODY WEIGHT IN YOUR APPLES AGAIN, AJ, I WOULDN'T CALL THE EFFECTS FROM THE LAST TIME AN ADVENTU—
APPLE ODYSSEY
DO NOT DISTURB!
NO, SILLY, THESE AREN'T FOR US. WE'RE GOING TO DELIVER THEM.
TO WHOM?
TO EVERYONE.
AND WHAT MAKES YOU THINK EVERYONE'S GOING TO...
...WANT...
I USED APPLES FROM THE CROP YOU SAVED. WE'VE GOT SOMETHING SPECIAL ON OUR HOOVES.
THIS IS DELICIOUS! A PONY COULD FORGET ABOUT FLYING AGAIN IF THESE WERE ON THE GROUND.
I DON'T KNOW HOW IT WORKED, BUT THESE APPLES ARE SOMETHING ELSE, RAINBOW. LITTLE SURPRISE WHEN THEY CAME FROM YOUR VERY BEST.
WHAT DO YOU WANT ME TO DO?
CATCH!
EASY, NEXT?
BRING IT BACK DOWN HERE.
DOWN...?

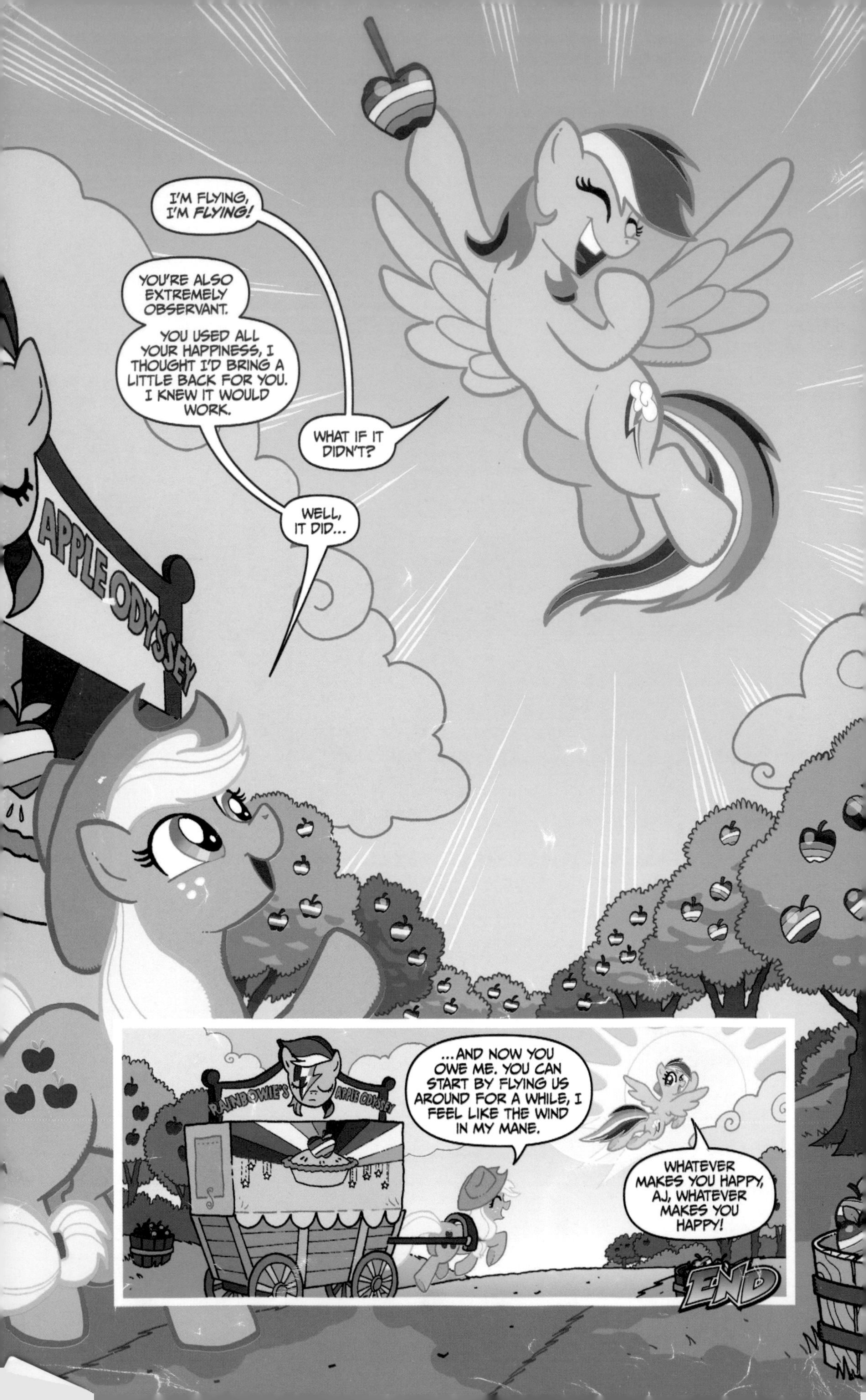
I'M FLYING, I'M FLYING!
YOU'RE ALSO EXTREMELY OBSERVANT.
YOU USED ALL YOUR HAPPINESS, I THOUGHT I'D BRING A LITTLE BACK FOR YOU. I KNEW IT WOULD WORK.
WHAT IF IT DIDN'T?
WELL, IT DID...
APPLE ODYSSEY
RAINBOWIE'S APPLE ODYSSEY
...AND NOW YOU OWE ME. YOU CAN START BY FLYING US AROUND FOR A WHILE, I FEEL LIKE THE WIND IN MY MANE.
WHATEVER MAKES YOU HAPPY, AJ, WHATEVER MAKES YOU HAPPY!
END